Within the fairy-tale treasure which has come into the world's possession, there is no doubt Hans Christian Andersen's stories are of outstanding character. Their symbolism is rich with Christian values, and some of them are clear illustrations of the Gospel. From his early childhood in the town of Odense, Denmark, until his death in Copenhagen, Hans Christian Andersen (1805-1875) had a valid Christian faith that manifested itself in many of the approximately 150 stories and tales he wrote. In one of them, he said: "In every human life, whether poor or great, there is an invisible thread that shows we belong to God." The thread in Andersen's stories is one of optimism which has given hope and inspiration to people all over the world.

It is in this spirit that the Tales of Hans Christian Andersen are published. We are convinced of the validity of teaching spiritual principles and building character values through imaginative stories, just as Jesus used parables to teach the people of His time.

THE WILD SWANS
by Hans Christian Andersen
Translated from the original Danish text by Marlee Alex
Illustrated by Juan Ramon Alonso Diaz-Toledo
U.S. edition 1988 by WORD Inc. Waco, TX 76702

Text: © Copyright 1984 Scandinavia Publishing House
Artwork: © Copyright 1984 J.R. Alonso Diaz-Toledo and Scandinavia Publishing House
Printed in Hong Kong
ISBN 0-8499-8538-2

The Wild Swans

Hans Christian Andersen

Illustrated by Juan Alonso Diaz-Toledo
Translated from the original text
by Marlee Alex

WORD INC.

Far, far away, where the swallows fly in the winter, lived a king who had eleven sons and one daughter, Elisa. When the eleven princes went to school, they wore stars on their chests and carried swords at their sides. They wrote on golden tablets with diamond pencils and could recite their lessons by heart. Their sister Elisa sat on a little chair made of solid glass and looked at a picture book that had cost half the kingdom.

The children were very fortunate, but it was not always to remain that way.

One day their father married a wicked queen, who was not at all good to the poor children. Things were different from the very first day.

The palace had been decorated, so the children played house in the courtyard. But instead of getting all the cakes and roasted apples they wished for, the queen gave them only sand in a teacup. She told them to make believe it was something nice.

A week later the queen sent Elisa to live with some peasants in the country, and it was not long before she had influenced the king so much that he no longer cared at all for the eleven princes.

8

"Fly out into the world and take care of yourselves!" screamed the wicked queen to the brothers. "Fly like great birds without voices!" But she was not able to put as terrible a curse on them as she wished to.

With a strange cry, eleven wild swans flew out of the palace windows and over the forest. While it was still early in the morning, they flew over the cottage where their sister Elisa was sleeping. Swerving over the roof top, they turned their long necks and flapped their wings, but no one heard or saw them. So away they flew, into the clouds and the wide world.

In the peasant cottage, poor little Elisa played with a leaf, for she had no other toys. She made a hole in the leaf and looked through it up at the sun. It reminded her of the bright eyes of her brothers. Each time the warm sunbeams shone on her cheeks she thought of all their kisses.

One day passed just like the other. The wind blew through the big rose hedge outside and whispered to the roses, "Who can be more beautiful than you?"

The roses shook their heads and answered, "Elisa is!"

On Sundays, the peasant woman sat in the doorway and read her hymn-book. The wind rippled the pages and said to the book, "Who can be more devout than you?"

"Elisa is," said the hymn-book. And it was perfectly true.

When she was fifteen years old, Elisa was brought home to the palace. The queen was angry and spiteful when she saw how beautiful Elisa had grown. She would have gladly changed her into a wild swan like her brothers, but she did not dare do this at once because the king wished to see his daughter.

Early one morning the queen went into the marble bathroom that was decorated with soft cushions and lush carpets. She took three toads with her, kissed them, and said to the first, "Sit on Elisa's head when she comes to bathe, so that she becomes lazy like you!" To the second she commanded, "Sit on her forehead, so that she becomes ugly and her father will not recognize her." To the third she whispered, "Rest upon her heart, so that she may be tormented by an evil mind." When the queen put the toads into the clear water, it turned green immediately.

The queen called Elisa and commanded her to go down into the water. When Elisa entered the bath the first toad sat in her hair, the second on her forehead, and the third on her breast. But Elisa seemed not to notice it. When she got out again, three red poppies floated on the water. If the toads had not been poisonous and kissed by the witch, then they would have become red roses instead. But by resting upon Elisa's head and heart, they had at least become flowers. She was so pure and innocent that the magic had no power over her.

When the wicked queen saw this, she rubbed Elisa's skin with walnut juice until it was streaked and stained. She smeared her beautiful face with a bad-smelling ointment and let it tangle her lovely hair. So it was quite impossible to recognize beautiful Elisa.

Her father exclaimed, "This girl cannot be my daughter!"

No one recognized Elisa except the dog and the swallows, but they were mere animals and so could not say a word. Elisa began to cry. She longed for her eleven brothers who were no longer there. Sadly, she slipped out of the palace and walked over the fields and through the marshland towards the forest.

11

She did not have the least idea where she was going. She was brokenhearted. She imagined that her brothers had probably been driven from the palace just as she had been, and she decided to look for them.

Elisa entered the forest only a short time before nightfall. Leaving the pathway, she lay down on the soft moss and said her evening prayer. It was very quiet. The air was warm, and around about the place where she lay, hundreds of glowworms shone like green firelight. When she softly touched one of the branches, the glowworms fell like shooting stars.

14

Throughout the night Elisa dreamed of her brothers. In her dreams they played again as children, wrote with diamond pencils on golden tablets, and looked at the picture book which had cost half the kingdom. But they did not merely draw numbers and sketches as they had before. Instead they wrote the loveliest poems about all they had done, seen, and heard. And in the picture book, everything was living. The birds sang aloud, and the people left the pages of the book and spoke to Elisa and her brothers. When she turned the pages, the people jumped in again so that the pictures would not get mixed up.

When Elisa awoke, the sun was already high in the sky and hidden behind the thick branches of the trees, but above her the rays of sunlight played around her like sprinkled gold dust. There was a fresh smell of greenery, and the birds fluttered near her shoulder. She heard water bubbling like a fountain, and, following the sound, came to a pond fed by many large springs. Thick bushes grew around it, but at one place deers had dug an opening. Elisa crawled through it down to the water.

The water in the pond was so clear that if the branches of the trees above had not been swaying with the wind, Elisa would have thought they were painted on the sandy bottom, for the water reflected each leaf in detail.

When Elisa saw the reflection of her own face in the water, she was frightened. It was so dirty and ugly! She rubbed her eyes and forehead with water until her skin finally shone through. Then she undressed and swam into the fresh water to bathe. A lovelier king's daughter could not be found anywhere in the whole world.

When she was dressed again and had plaited her long hair, she went over to the bubbling spring and scooped the fresh water into her mouth and then wandered farther into the forest. She thought about her brothers and about her loving Lord, who surely would not forsake her. It was He who had made wild apple trees to feed the hungry, and who now led her to just such a tree with branches weighed down with fruit. Here she ate lunch, put props under the tree's branches, and then continued into the darkest part of the forest.

It was so quiet she could hear the sound of her own footsteps and the crunch of each little withered leaf beneath her feet. There was not a single bird to be seen, not a beam of light penetrating the large, intertwining tree branches. The tree trunks were so close that it was as if she were shut in by a fence. She felt a loneliness she had never known before.

The night was very dark. Not a single glowworm shone in the moss.
Sadly, she lay down to sleep. And then it seemed to her that the tree branches parted above her and the Lord Himself looked down at her with gentle eyes. Little angels were peeking over His head and under His arms. When she awoke in the morning she did not know if it had been a dream, or if it had really happened.

She had not gone far when she met an old woman who gave her some berries from a basket. Elisa asked if she had seen eleven princes riding through the forest.

"No," said the old woman, "but yesterday I saw eleven swans, wearing golden crowns swimming in the stream close to here."

The woman led Elisa to a bank over a curving stream. The trees on the shore spread their long, leafy branches over the water towards each other. And where they could not reach, they had pulled their roots out of the soil to lean farther across.

Elisa said goodbye to the old woman and walked beside the stream until she came to an open beach. The great ocean lay before the young girl, but there was not a boat or ship in sight. How was she to go farther? She studied the countless small pebbles on the beach. The water had worn them round and smooth. Glass, iron, stones - everything that had been washed ashore had received their shape and form from the constant movements of the water, which was far softer than even her delicate hand.

"The ocean is tireless at polishing these hard stones. I will be just as tireless! Thank you for your wisdom, rolling waves! My heart tells me that one day you will carry me to my dear brothers."

Among the seaweed that had been washed ashore lay eleven white swan feathers. Elisa gathered them into a bouquet. There were drops of water on them; whether they were drops of dew or teardrops, no one could tell.

It was lonesome along the beach, but Elisa did not feel lonely, for the ocean was constantly changing, more than the inland lakes did in an entire year. If a large cloud rolled over, it was as if the ocean wanted to say: "I can also look dark and angry." Then the wind blew, and the waves turned their white side out. If the sky was red and the wind slept, the ocean was soft as a rose petal. But no matter how quietly the ocean rested, there was always gentle movement along the beach as the water softly heaved like the breast of a sleeping child.

When the sun was close to setting, Elisa saw eleven wild swans wearing golden crowns flying towards land. They glided one after the other like a long, white ribbon. Elisa climbed upon the cliff and hid behind a bush. The swans landed close to her, flapping their magnificent wings.

As the sun sank below the water, their swan feathers fell away suddenly, and there stood eleven princes, Elisa's brothers. She cried out in joy, for even though they had changed, she knew it was them; it could only be them! She jumped into their arms and called them by name. They were overjoyed when they recognized their little sister, who had now grown up to be so beautiful. They laughed and cried and it was not long before Elisa and her brothers realized how wickedly their stepmother had treated them all.

The eldest brother explained, "We fly as wild swans as long as the sun stays in the sky. When it disappears we become human again. We have to be sure to be on land at sunset, for if we were flying, we would fall to our deaths. We live in a country just as beautiful as this on the other side of the ocean. It is a great distance from here, and there are no islands on the way where we can stop for the night, except for a lonely little rock sticking up in the middle of the sea. The rock is just large enough for us to stand side by side while we rest. If the sea is rough, water sprays over us. But we thank God for it, otherwise, we could never come here to visit our dear fatherland.

"We use the two longest days of the year to make our flight and can stay here only eleven days each year. We fly over the castle where we were born and where Father still lives, and over the church where Mother is buried. It seems as if the wild life and trees here are our family. We watch the wild horses run over the plains, and listen to the gypsies' songs that we danced to as children. We are drawn to return here, and now we have found you, our dear little sister. We can stay only two days longer before we fly over the sea again. How can we take you with us? We have neither ship nor boat."

"If only I could set you free from this curse!" said Elisa.

That night Elisa and her brothers talked for hours, sleeping very little.

Elisa was awakened at dawn by the sound of swan wings rushing above her. Her brothers circled overhead and flew away, leaving the youngest behind. He laid his head in Elisa's lap while she stroked his wings. The two of them stayed together all day until the others returned. When the sun set, the swans were men again.

"Tomorrow we shall fly away and not return for a whole year, but we could never leave you behind. Do you have the courage to go with us? If the arms of one of us are strong enough to carry you through the forest, should not our wings be strong enough together to carry you over the ocean?"

"Yes, take me with you!" exclaimed Elisa.

Elisa's brothers spent the night braiding a large, strong net of soft reeds and willow bark. Elisa fell asleep upon it. When the sun rose and the brothers were changed to wild swans, they took the net in their beaks and flew high into the clouds with their sleeping sister. The sunbeams fell onto her face, so one of the swans flew over her head, spreading his wings above her for shade.

They were far from land when Elisa woke up. She thought she was dreaming, for it was strange to be carried high through the air over the ocean. Beside her lay a branch with delicious ripe berries and a bunch of sweet-smelling roots that the youngest brother had gathered for her. She smiled thankfully to him, for she knew it was he who was flying over her head and shading her with his wings.

They were so high that the first ship they saw beneath them looked like a seagull sitting on the water. The cloud behind them resembled a huge mountain, and Elisa watched the shadows of herself and her eleven brothers fly across it like giants. It was a sight more wonderful than any she had ever seen before. As the sun grew higher and the cloud moved farther behind them, the moving shadow picture disappeared.

All day long they flew as an arrow rushing through the air. Actually, they were slower than usual, since they had their little sister to carry. Evening grew close, and Elisa watched the sun sink with fear in her heart. The lonely rock in the ocean was not to be seen. The swans were beating their wings harder and harder. Elisa knew it was her fault that they had not made better time. She prayed to God in the depths of her heart, but still she did not spy the rock.

Black clouds closed in around them, strong gusts of wind foretold a storm, lightning flashed against the sky again and again. The sun was now on the edge of the sea, and Elisa's heart trembled. Suddenly, the swans dove downward. She thought they were falling until they began to glide again. When the sun was half-way below the horizon she spied the little rock beneath them. It looked no larger than a seal pup sticking his head up above the waves.

The sun sank quickly until it was only a star, then Elisa's foot touched the ground. The last spark of the sun went out like a bit of burning paper. Arm in arm Elisa's brothers stood around her as the waves beat against the rock. The heavens were shining like fire, and the thunder rolled. Elisa and her brothers held hands and sang a hymn that comforted and encouraged them.

At dawn the air was quiet. As soon as the sun rose, the swans flew away again with Elisa. The ocean was still rough. From high in the air the white foam on the black-green waves looked like millions of floating swans.

As the sun grew higher, Elisa saw before her a mountainous land crowned by shining ice caps. In the center, above a beach of waving palm trees and flowers as large as mill wheels, stood a mile long castle, with row upon row of magnificent towers. She asked if that were the country for which they were heading, but the swans shook their heads. What she saw was in reality the Morning Princess's constantly changing castle of clouds. The swans did not dare to bring a human there.

As Elisa stared at it, the mountains crumbled, the castle collapsed, and in their places, stood twenty proud churches, exactly alike, with high towers and pointed windows. She thought she heard the organ playing, but it was only the ocean. As they drew near, the churches took on the appearance of a fleet of ships sailing below. It was really the ocean fog rolling over the water. Before her eyes everything was eternally changing.

Then Elisa saw the real land. They came upon a lovely blue mountain covered with cedar forests, villages and castles. Long before the sun went down she sat on the mountainside, in front of a large cave overgrown with green vines. It looked like an embroidered tapestry. "Now we shall see what you will dream of tonight!" said the youngest brother as he showed her to her bed-chamber.

"If only I might dream of how I could rescue you!" she answered. The thought of it captivated her mind and heart. She prayed earnestly to God for help, and kept on praying as she fell asleep.

In her dreams Elisa flew through the air to the castle of the Morning Princess, where a beautiful, glittering fairy met her. The fairy resembled the old woman who had given her berries in the forest and told her about the eleven swans wearing golden crowns.

"Your brothers can be rescued!" the fairy promised. "But do you have courage and endurance? The ocean is softer than your hands and yet can transform the hardest stones. But it does not feel the pain your fingers will feel. It has no heart and does not suffer the fear and anxiety which you must endure.

"Do you see these nettles I hold in my hand? There are many such nettles growing around the cave where you are sleeping. Only these and the ones growing in churchyards can be used. Remember that.

Although they will sting until blisters appear, you must pick the nettles and crush them with your feet into flax, then knit eleven long-sleeved shirts. When you throw these shirts over the eleven wild swans, the curse will be broken. But remember, from the moment you begin the task until it is finished, though years may pass, you must not speak. The first word you say will drive a knife into your brothers' hearts. The lives of your brothers depend upon your tongue."

The fairy touched Elisa's hand with nettles that stung like little flames, and Elisa woke up. It was daylight, and close beside her lay a nettle like the one she had seen in the dream. She fell on her knees, gave thanks to God, and went outside to begin her work. Her delicate hands grabbed the stinging nettles. They burned like fire and blistered her hands and arms, but she suffered the pain gladly, thinking only of salvation for her dear brothers. She crushed each nettle with her bare feet and spun them into green twine.

After sunset Elisa's brothers returned to the cave and were frightened at finding her unable to speak. They thought it must be due to a new curse of their evil stepmother. But when they saw her hands, they understood that what she was doing was for their sake. The youngest brother cried, and where his tears fell, the pain and the blisters disappeared.

All night long Elisa worked, for she would never have peace of heart before she had set her brothers free. All the next day, while the swans were away, she sat alone. But time had never flown so quickly. She finished one shirt and began on the next.

Suddenly, the sound of a hunter's horn rang through the mountains. Elisa grew afraid. As the sound of barking dogs came closer, she hurried into the cave, tying the nettles she had gathered into a bundle. At that moment a large dog jumped out of the thicket, followed by another, and another. They barked loudly and ran back and forth. Before long the hunters stood before the opening to the cave. The most handsome among them was the king. He stepped into the cave and saw Elisa. Never had he seen a more beautiful girl.

"What are you doing here, you lovely child?" he asked. Elisa shook her head. She dared not speak, for the lives of her brothers depended on it. She hid her hands under her apron so the king would not see how she suffered.

"Follow me!" he commanded. "You must not stay here. If you are as sweet as you are beautiful, I will have you dressed in silk and velvet, and have a golden crown set on your head. You shall live in my royal palace."

He lifted Elisa onto his horse. She cried and wrung her hands, but the king explained, "I only want to make you happy. One day you will thank me for it!" And he rode away through the mountains, holding her in front of him on the horse. The other hunters followed closely behind.

As the sun set, a majestic city with its churches and towers came into sight. The king led Elisa into the palace where the waters of a large fountain splashed into pools. Both the walls and ceiling of the palace were covered with paintings. But Elisa did not notice them, for she was crying in sorrow. Passively, she allowed the women to dress her in royal robes, braid pearls into her hair, and pull dainty gloves over her blistered fingers.

When she finally appeared in all her finery, she was so beautiful that the court bowed deeply before her. The king proposed to make her his bride. But the archbishop shook his head, saying that the beautiful girl from the woods was probably a witch who had blinded their eyes and bewitched the heart of the king.

The king did not listen to him. He commanded music to be played, and that there should be feasting and dancing for Elisa. He led Elisa through the fragrant gardens and great rooms of the palace. However, not a smile crossed Elisa's lips, nor shone from her eyes.

There was only sorrow painted upon her face. Then the king showed her to a small chamber decorated with green carpets and wallpaper. It resembled the cave where he had found her. On the floor lay the bundle of twine she had spun from the nettles, and from the ceiling hung the finished shirt. The hunters had taken it with them as a curiosity.

"Here you can dream yourself back to your former home!" said the king. "Here is the task that kept you busy. In the splendor of the palace it may amuse you to think back on your past."

When Elisa saw that which was so dear to her heart, a smile played about her lips and the blood returned to her cheeks. She thought again of the salvation of her brothers and kissed the hand of the king as he drew her to his heart. All the church bells rang out, proclaiming the wedding celebration. The lovely, silent girl from the woods was to become the queen.

The archbishop whispered evil words into the king's ear, but they did not penetrate his heart. The wedding was to take place, and the archbishop himself was to set the crown on Elisa's head. He pressed the crown harshly upon her forehead until it hurt. But the sorrow she felt for her brothers was far more painful.

Elisa did not speak, but her eyes glowed with a deep love for the good and handsome king who did all he could to make her happy. She became more and more fond of him. If only she dared to confide in him and tell him why she suffered! But silent she must remain, silently she must fulfill her task. At night she quietly left his side, went into her little chamber, and knitted one shirt after another. When she began the seventh, she ran out of twine. The nettles she needed grew in the churchyard, but how could she dare go out to gather them?

"Oh, what is the pain in my fingers compared to that in my heart?" she thought. "I must take the risk! The Lord will not fail me!"

With fear in her heart, as if it were an evil deed she was planning, she slipped out into the moonlit night, walked through the long winding alleys, out onto the empty streets, and towards the churchyard. When she arrived she saw a group of hideous witches sitting on one of the gravestones. They were taking their tattered clothes off, and with long, lean fingers were digging into the earth. Elisa had to pass right by them. They fastened their eyes upon her, but she whispered a prayer, gathered the nettles, and hurried back to the palace.

Only one person had seen her, the Archbishop. Now he was confirmed in his suspicions that she was a witch who had deceived the king and court. The following day, he told the king from the confession booth what he had seen and what he had feared. When the hard words fell from his tongue, the carved statues of the saints shook their heads as if they wanted to say, "It is not so, Elisa is innocent." But the archbishop interpreted this to mean just the opposite, that they were witnessing against her and shaking their heads at her evil witchcraft.

Two heavy tears rolled down the king's cheeks. He went home with doubt in his heart and only pretended to sleep that night. He noticed that Elisa got up out of bed and disappeared into her green chamber. She repeated this every night, and each time he secretly followed her.

Day by day the king's expression became darker. Elisa saw it, but did not understand why. It worried her, and she worried as well for her brothers. Her salty tears fell on the purple velvet gown she wore and glittered like diamonds. Everyone who saw this exquisite sight wished they could be a queen too.

Soon Elisa would be finished with her task. Only one shirt remained to be made, but she had no more twine and not a single nettle. Once again, for the last time, she would have to go to the churchyard and pick more of them. She remembered fearfully the lonely walk and the frightful witches. But her will was set, as was her confidence in the Lord.

As Elisa left the palace, the king and the archbishop followed and watched her disappear through the gate into the churchyard. When they drew closer they saw the witches as Elisa had seen them. The king turned his face away, for he imagined that his beloved, whose head had rested upon his chest that very evening, was going to join their company.

"The people must judge her!" he exclaimed.

And the people declared, "She shall be burned at the stake!"

From the splendid palace, Elisa was led into a dark, damp cell where the wind whistled through the barred windows. She was given the bunch of nettles she had gathered for a pillow, and the stiff, burning shirts she had knitted for a blanket. But nothing more precious could have been given to her. She took up her task again as she prayed to God. Outside, the boys in the street sang mocking songs about her. Not a soul comforted her with a single kind word.

At the close of the day a swan wing appeared at the barred window. It was the youngest of the brothers, who had found his sister. Elisa wept aloud for joy, even though she knew the coming night was perhaps to be her last. All that mattered now was that her task was almost finished and that her brothers were with her. The Archbishop came to be with Elisa for the last hour of her life, just as he had promised the king. But Elisa shook her head at him and begged in sign language to be left alone. She must finish her work or everything would be in vain; the pain, the tears, the sleepless nights.

The archbishop left with evil words about her, but Elisa knew she was innocent and remained at her task. Little mice ran over the floor and helped by dragging the nettles to her feet. The thrush perched at the window-bars, and sang bravely throughout the night to keep her courage up.

At dawn, less than an hour before the sunrise, Elisa's brothers stood at the gates of the palace, and demanded to be led before the king. They were refused permission on the grounds that the king could not be disturbed. They begged and they threatened until the king himself came out. But at that moment the sun rose, and Elisa's brothers were no longer there. The king saw only eleven wild swans flying low over the palace.

Townspeople streamed through the city gates, intending to see the burning of the witch. A scraggly old horse pulled the cart upon which she sat. She was dressed in rough sackcloth, and her lovely long hair hung loose around her beautiful face. Her cheeks were deathly pale, but her lips moved gently as her fingers continued to knit the green twine. Even on the way to her death she refused to give up her task. Ten shirts lay at her feet as she continued on the eleventh.

The crowd jeered. "Look at the witch, see how she mumbles! She carries no hymn-book in her hand but only her gruesome witchcraft! Tear it from her hands and into a thousand pieces!"

The crowd pressed close to the cart and would have grabbed the nettle shirt, but eleven white swans appeared and flew at them. The swans sat around Elisa on the cart and flapped their powerful wings, forcing the mob to the side.

"It is a sign from Heaven. She must be innocent," whispered many. But they did not dare to say it aloud.

As the executioner grabbed her by the hand, she quickly threw the eleven shirts over the swans. Suddenly in their places stood eleven princes. The youngest, however, had a swan wing instead of an arm, for Elisa had not had time to finish the last sleeve of his shirt.

"Now I may speak!" Elisa cried out. "I am innocent!"

The people who had watched what happened, knelt before her as before a saint. But Elisa sank lifeless into the arms of her brothers. The fear, worry, and pain had taken all her strength.

"Yes, she is innocent!" shouted the oldest brother. He told everything that had happened, and while he spoke a fragrance floated through the air. It was like the perfume of a million roses. Every piece of kindling at the stake had taken root and sent forth branches, until it became a sweet-smelling hedge covered with red roses. At the top a single white rose bloomed, shining and radiant as a star.

The king picked it and laid it on Elisa's breast. Straight away she awoke and her heart was filled with peace and happiness.

All the church bells started ringing by themselves, and birds flew above them in large flocks. It was a bridal procession back to the palace as no king as ever seen.

8/01